Santa's New Jet

David Biedrzycki

ini Charlesbridge

"Felis Nabidat" to all my friends in
Guam—Jen Woodard, Aimee Lizama,
Cyndy Pruski, Vickie Loughran,
Monique Stone, Bea Camacho,
and Tina Buendicho

First Charlesbridge edition 2011
Copyright © 2007 by David Biedrzycki

Published by Charlesbridge
85 Main Street
Watertown, MA 02472
(617) 926-0329
www.charlesbridge.com

Library of Congress Cataloging-in-Publication Data
Biedrzycki, David.
    Santa's new jet / David Biedrzycki
        p. cm.
    Summary: Shortly before Christmas, Santa discovers that the sleigh needs major repairs
and the reindeer are out of shape, and so the elves build him a jet to use on his annual trip.
    ISBN 978-1-58089-291-9 (reinforced for library use)
    ISBN 978-1-58089-292-6 (softcover)
[1. Santa Claus—Fiction. 2. Elves—Fiction.
3. Jet planes—Fiction. 4. Christmas—Fiction. 5. Humorous stories.]
I. Title.
PZ7.B4745San 2011
[E]—dc22   2010041824

Printed in China
(hc) 10 9 8 7 6 5 4 3 2 1
(sc) 10 9 8 7 6 5 4 3 2 1

Illustrations done in Photoshop
Display type and text type set in Hunniwell Bold and Animated Gothic Heavy
Color separations by Chroma Graphics, Singapore
Printed and bound February 2011 by Jade Productions in Heyuan, Guangdong, China
Production supervision by Brian G. Walker
Designed by David Biedrzycki and Connie Brown

Christmas Eve was coming.
It was time to get ready for the big night.

The sleigh needed work—a lot of work.

I went to get the reindeer.

They were out of shape . . .

. . . really out of shape.

It was time to practice.

Practice was less than perfect.

It wasn't looking good for Christmas,
but Orville the elf had an idea.

Orville said the elves could build
me a jet to deliver the toys.
I liked his plan.

The elves worked their magic, and the next day I had a jet—in my favorite color,

with an extra-wide seat,

that was easy to use, and had many safety features.

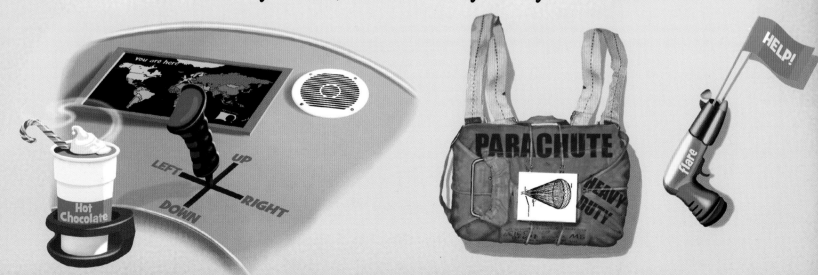

I took the jet out for a spin.

The elves waved, but I wondered where the reindeer were.

The jet was fast, and it carried lots of toys.

I could fly with the top up

or the top down.

On Christmas Eve the elves helped
me pack the jet and off I went.

The jet was noisy, and the onboard computer kept telling me where to go. The voice sounded just like Mrs. Claus!

It is now
12:01 am.
Do you know
where your
reindeer are?

Slow down!

Take a left at
Hawaii.
If you have time
stop and get me a
fresh
pineapple.

I missed the reindeer and their gentle sleigh bells.

I also missed landing on the
first, second, third, and fourth roofs.
On the fifth roof, I woke everyone up.
The reindeer were *never* this loud.

Blitzen had always been good at telling me what toys to leave.

But at the next stop, I just pumped toys from the jet into the house. It was easy—maybe too easy.

Later, fog set in and I couldn't see.
I needed Rudolph to light the way.

I was falling behind, and it was almost
Christmas morning.

I used the flare
to signal for help.

The reindeer saw my SOS all the way up at the North Pole.

They hitched themselves up, and away they flew.

They found me in no time.

The reindeer were in great shape, and the sleigh had never looked better.

The History of Flight Museum

The reindeer did their work quietly,
and Christmas was saved.

I wonder what they
were thinking about.